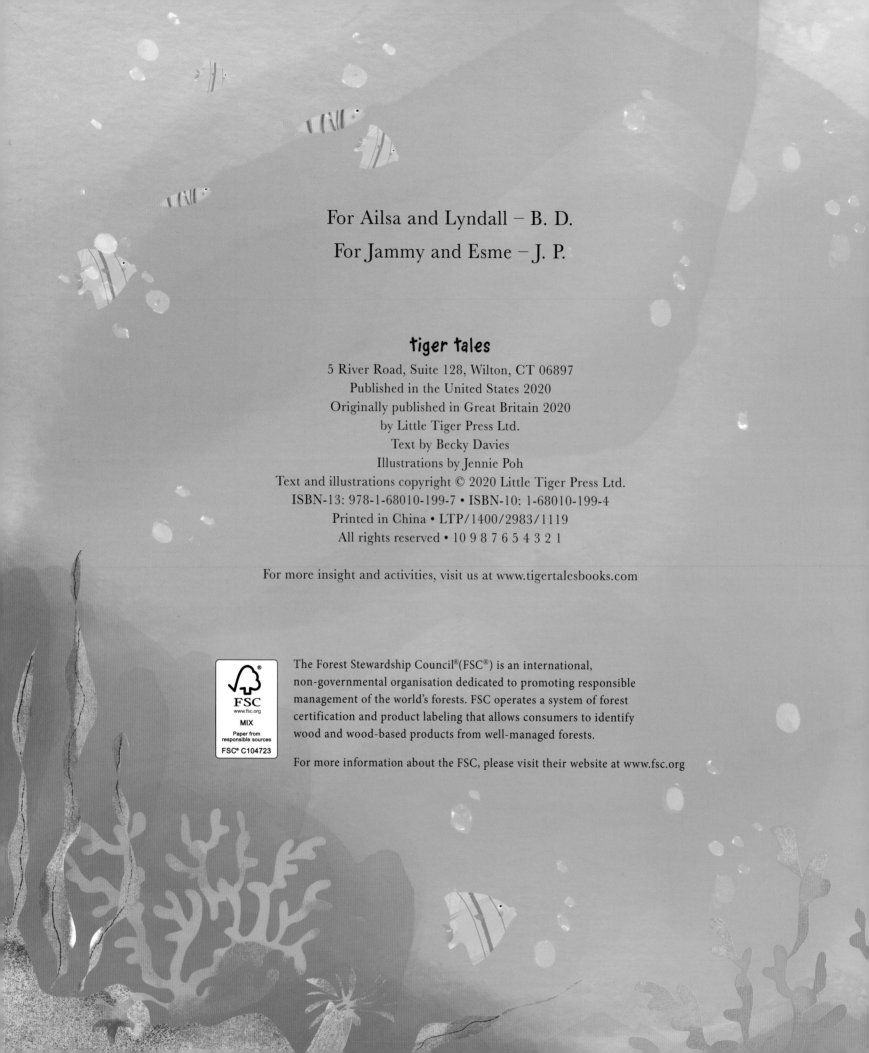

For Ailsa and Lyndall – B. D.

For Jammy and Esme – J. P.

tiger tales

5 River Road, Suite 128, Wilton, CT 06897

Published in the United States 2020

Originally published in Great Britain 2020

by Little Tiger Press Ltd.

Text by Becky Davies

Illustrations by Jennie Poh

Text and illustrations copyright © 2020 Little Tiger Press Ltd.

ISBN-13: 978-1-68010-199-7 • ISBN-10: 1-68010-199-4

Printed in China • LTP/1400/2983/1119

All rights reserved • 10 9 8 7 6 5 4 3 2 1

For more insight and activities, visit us at www.tigertalesbooks.com

The Forest Stewardship Council®(FSC®) is an international, non-governmental organisation dedicated to promoting responsible management of the world's forests. FSC operates a system of forest certification and product labeling that allows consumers to identify wood and wood-based products from well-managed forests.

For more information about the FSC, please visit their website at www.fsc.org

Little Turtle
and the
Changing Sea

by Becky Davies

Illustrated by Jennie Poh

tiger tales

It began with a thunderstorm.

The rain lashed and the waves crashed as
Little Turtle pushed her way out of the
nest and onto the wet sand.

She needed to be quick. One flipper in
front of the other, she pulled herself down
the beach toward the safety of the sea.

Thunder rumbled in the sky as Little Turtle slipped into the sea for the very first time. The water rose to meet her, and she was tossed and turned in the spray.

Which way was up? Tiny turtles splashed all around her, calling, "Swim, swim!"

Just when Little Turtle's flippers were tiring,
she managed to hitch a ride.

Her journey had begun!

Warm currents carried
Little Turtle over a carpet
of color.

She danced with the swaying
seagrass. She swam with fish
of every shape and size.

"What beauty!" she said.
Happy and content, Little Turtle
climbed into a cozy hole in a
rock and slept.

Months passed, and Turtle
was no longer little.

She had outgrown her
hideway . . .

. . . but she would never outgrow the ocean. Turtle swam onward through miles of dazzling open water.

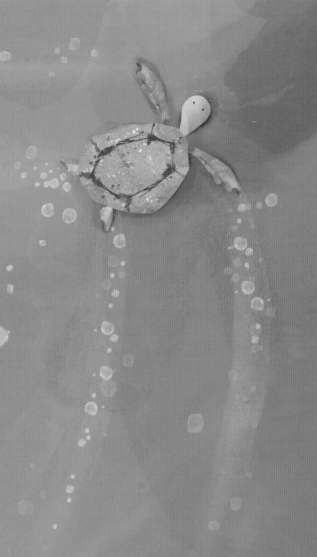

She was alone, but she didn't feel lonely.

The ocean was her friend.

At last, Turtle's journey was complete. She had made it to the other side of the world.

"Home," sighed Turtle.

And what a home it was!

Foraging and feeding, Turtle lived there happily for many years.

Until one day, it was time for her to return . . .

. . . to the beach across the
ocean where she had been born.
She made this same journey
many times but found that each
time, the trip was different.

Turtle, too, was different. As she
grew each year, her love for the
ocean grew with her.

She saw new sights, made new friends, and welcomed some new little turtles into the world.

Then one day, the ocean itself was different.

Colors disappeared, and Turtle found strange new creatures swimming beside her.

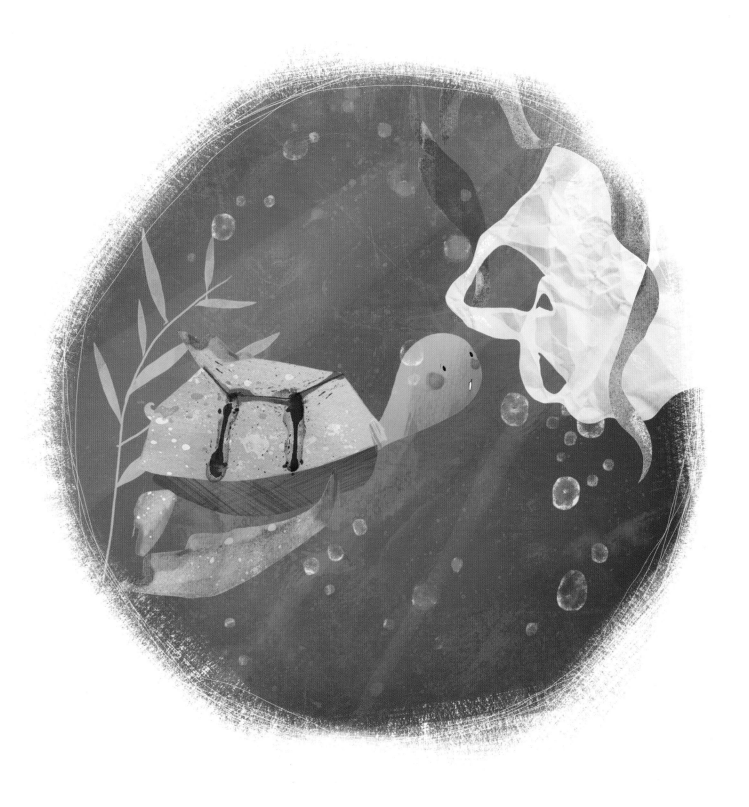

"Friend?" she asked. But she was met with silence.

The strangeness
grew and grew.

And Turtle felt lost in
the place she knew most.

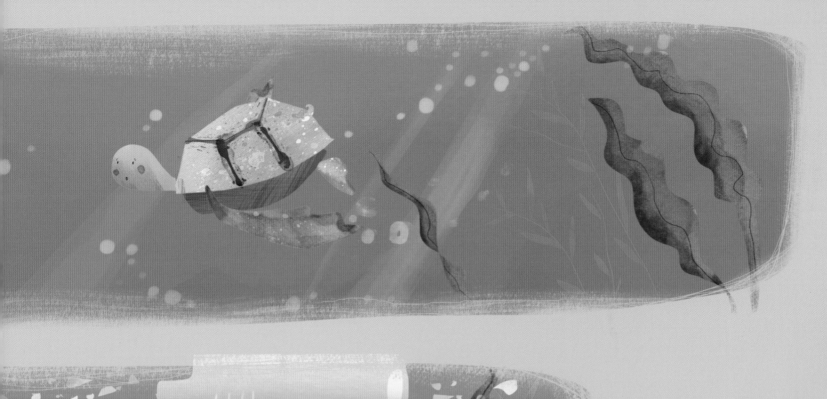

Nothing looked

the same . . . .

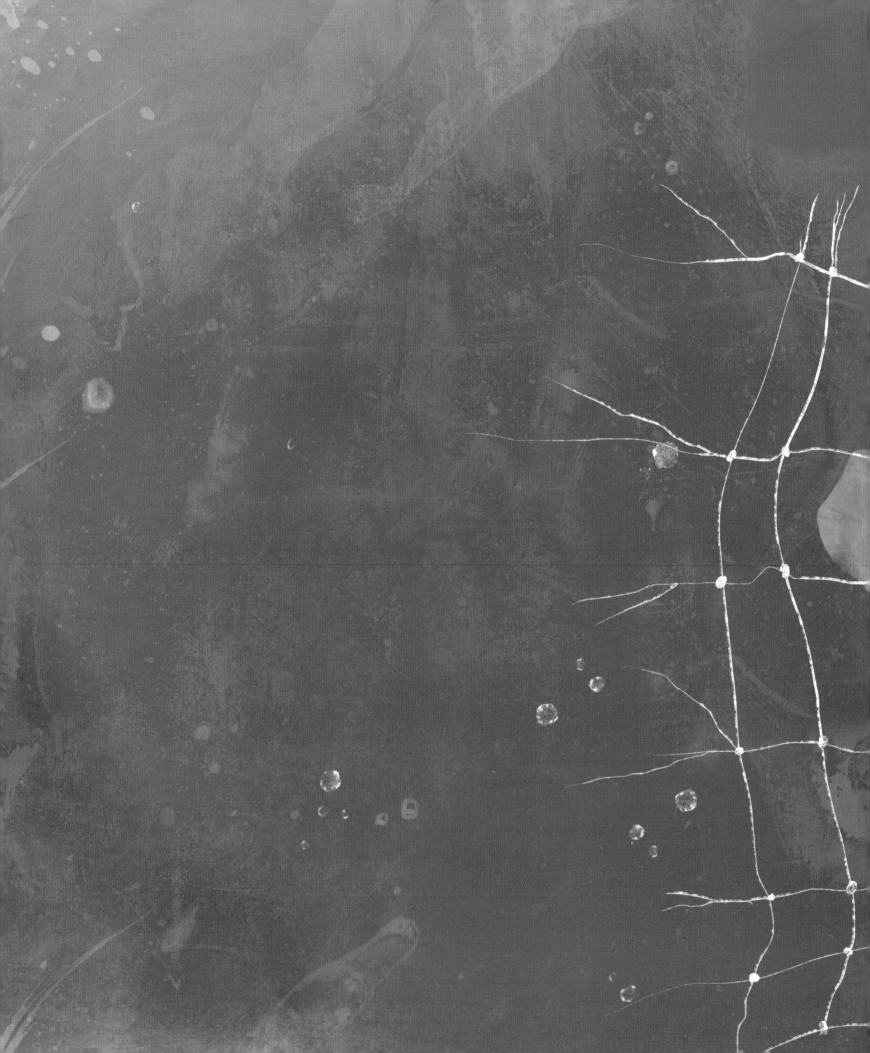

The ocean no longer felt like a friend.

"Hello?" she spoke into the darkness.

But Turtle was alone.

Just when Turtle thought
her journey was over forever,
figures emerged from the
strangeness and swam
toward her.

Turtle was free!

Little by little, she watched as they tended to the seagrass, the coral, and her friends. Then they cleaned up the garbage.

"Thank you," she said. They had returned her to the ocean . . .

. . . and began to return Turtle's ocean to her.
It was beautiful once more, and she loved it
with her whole heart.

Note from the author

I've loved the ocean ever since I was little, when my family would take me on camping trips to Cornwall, England, and we'd beach-hop our way around the county. It was a visit to Newquay in Cornwall that inspired me to write the story of Little Turtle, after I met a blind turtle named Omiros at an aquarium.

Omiros was rescued in Greece after being found tangled in fishing nets. His tank is big and roomy, but because of the damage to his eyes, Omiros can never return home to the sea. All because of humans! Omiros is incredibly lucky, but I wonder if he knows what he's lost. Does he remember the ocean?

Our seas are steadily filling up with garbage and plastic. Beautiful coral reefs are disappearing, and sea creatures all around the world are losing their homes. But it's not too late to do something about it—and all of us can help.

Glossary of terms

Biodegradable: When something is biodegradable, it means that when thrown away, it breaks down into something already found in nature. If a material is not biodegradable, it will exist on Earth for a very long time!

Conserve: Protect something from being used up or harmed.

Coral: Corals are sea animals that stay in one place. Some types of coral build cases or skeletons that stay in the ocean after they die. After millions of years of growth, these cases form huge coral reefs, which then provide homes to other sea creatures.

Landfill: A place where garbage is buried in the ground.

Microplastic: Tiny pieces of plastic that don't break down. Sometimes they're so small that you can't even see them with your eyes—only under a microscope!

Pollution: Gases, smoke, and chemicals that lead to unhealthy air, water, or soil.

The Three Rs

Reduce: Cut down on the amount of garbage that we throw away.

Reuse: Give bags, bottles, and other waste a second life by using them again, or . . .

Recycle: . . . make them into something new!

The plastic problem

When we throw plastic away instead of **recycling** it, it stays on Earth for a very long time. This is because plastic isn't usually **biodegradable**. If plastic gets put into **landfills**, it can take up a lot of space, but it's worse if the plastic gets into our oceans—and it does!

How does garbage get into the ocean?

1. Down the drain. Drains lead to the ocean, so anything we flush, like wet wipes, cotton swabs, and dental floss, can end up in the sea.

2. Littering—and not just on the beach. Where does garbage on the street go? Much of it is collected, but it can be blown or washed into rivers and drains.

3. From the trash can. When garbage is taken to landfills, it is often blown away because it's so light.

The Great Garbage Patch

The Great Garbage Patch is a HUGE accumulation of garbage in the Pacific Ocean. It's an area the size of the United States, Mexico, and Central America put together! A lot of this garbage comes from plastic like plastic bags, bottle caps, water bottles, and Styrofoam cups. But some of it is so small you can barely see it, and this makes cleaning it up really difficult! This swirling mess of **microplastics** is incredibly dangerous to sea creatures. Groups like The Ocean Cleanup are doing everything they can to get rid of this garbage

How plastic hurts marine life

They eat it—Loggerhead sea turtles often mistake plastic bags for their favorite food—sea jellies! Other sea creatures and birds confuse different plastics for food, and when they eat it, their insides are damaged, and they can die. Microplastics are so small that fish can eat them accidentally!

They get stuck in it—Seals, turtles, and sea birds can get tangled in plastic fishing nets and bags, and they can't get free. Many sea animals have also become stuck in the plastic rings used to hold packs of drink cans together.

How long does it last? Follow the timeline to find out.

Apple core and
Cardboard box
2 months

Plastic bag
10-20 years

Plastic straw
200 years

What YOU can do to help!

Recycle as many cans, bottles, and bags as you can.

Don't litter.

Drink tap water instead of bottled.

Only use a plastic bag if you really need one, and try to reuse it.

Reuse things you would usually throw away.

Don't use plastic straws, plates, or cutlery.

Try to choose or buy things that don't have plastic wrapping.

Join a local litter cleanup event!

Plastic water bottle
450 years

Plastic drink rings
400 years

Further reading

Mission: Sea Turtle Rescue: All About Sea Turtles and How to Save Them,
Karen Romano Young, National Geographic Children's Books, 2015

Somebody Swallowed Stanley, Sarah Roberts and Hannah Peck,
Scholastic, 2019

The Sea Book, Charlotte Milner, DK Children, 2019

What a Waste: Trash, Recycling, and Protecting our Planet,
Jess French, DK Children, 2019

Online resources:

https://kids.nationalgeographic.com/explore/nature/
kids-vs-plastic/pollution

https://www.epa.gov/students/planet-protectors-activities-kids

https://nmssanctuaries.blob.core.windows.net/
sanctuaries-prod/media/archive/education/
pdfs/ogab.pdf

Parents, be sure to head over to this website for more
information on the Great Garbage Patch cleanup!

https://theoceancleanup.com